the good girl

part one

Cover Image
Mayer George/Shutterstock.com

ISBN: 978-0-9862933-4-4 [Print]

To my first loves
God
Mommy and Dad

Acknowledgements

Thanks to the Fling Box Set Writers for asking me to be a part of a great project. It's because of them, I was able to give birth to some really great characters in Gabriella and Phillippe.

Thanks to my Editor Jeanne Cadeau and eFormatter L.K. Campbell.

about the author

Tracy is a woman who loves God, Cute Guys and Fashion. Sometimes those last two things fight for second place, when there's a great designer sale.

She calls herself a partial New Yorker due to the two and half years she lived there. She refers to her books as Edgy Christian Fiction with real characters in real life situations. Like her characters, she's a small business owner waiting on that one cute guy, who loves God and understands her love of fashion.

To learn more about Tracy and her books go to
www.readtracyreed.com

Enjoy!
Tracy Reed

the good girl

part one

TRACY REED

chapter one

gabriella

I CONSIDER MYSELF TO BE smart. After all, I got my Bachelor's degree in three years, thanks to no social life, Summer school, and an extra load of classes. While my classmates were going to parties and football games, I was going to my internship.

I was fortunate to intern at Morgan Grant Holdings my senior year. I really like the company and the people. However, when I graduated and applied for a position, the only thing available was a Floating Assistant. I took it, because I know the company's policy is to promote from within. My parents don't understand why I'm so desperate to work for this company. I honestly don't understand it either. All I know is, it just feels right.

Morgan Grant has branches all over the world. I'm hoping wherever I land, I'll have the opportunity to travel and really make an impact. Since I've been floating, I've worked in nearly every department at their San Francisco headquarters.

I look at my job as a very long training program. During my internship, I was relegated to Mergers and Acquisitions. I liked the high powered energy and seeing deals go from inception to birth. However, as a floater, I loved the two weeks I was in Advertising. The creative energy there is like a drug. I love how they function as a group. If given the choice, that's where I'd like to be. Advertising works with all the departments and subsidiaries in all the offices. Creativity and travel…that's what I want. Until then, I'll keep floating and interviewing.

The Director of Human Resources called me early this morning, requesting I report to her office immediately for a special assignment. I quickly got dressed and headed to work.

I walked into her office and sat down. She handed me a card with only an office number. Before she could give me instructions, her computer dinged and she looked at the screen. After reading the screen, she grabbed her head, started typing and told me to go to the office upstairs and someone would give me details.

I took the elevator up to the twenty-third floor to the office number on the card. I've never worked on the Senior Executive floor. Most of the offices on this floor belong to the "big boys"…at least that's what I've heard.

The elevator stopped, the doors opened and my mouth dropped open. It was beautiful. It didn't look like an office, but like someone's luxurious living room. I looked around for a receptionist, but didn't see one. Maybe that's what I was going to be doing. I looked down at the card and it said twenty-three forty-two. I looked around and there were three doors. I searched for twenty-three forty-two and spotted the brushed steel numbers on the wall next to a hall. I walked down the long hall and stopped at the door marked, twenty-three forty-two.

I knocked on the door, but there was no answer. I turned the knob and the door opened. I walked inside and looked around the beautifully decorated black and white office with a view of the city. None of the spaces I've worked in had a window. Most of the offices with windows were reserved for executives. I thought to myself, "Whoever works in here probably prefers working at night with the lights of the city casting a sense of calm."

The walls were painted a beautiful glossy dark black. The white lacquered Parsons desk fit perfectly in the black and white space. However, the desk chair seemed out of place. It was as if whoever decorated the space forgot the assistant needed a chair, and grabbed the first thing they saw in storage. In front of the desk were two French-style arm chairs painted black with wide black and white stripe fabric. The only things on the desk were a vintage-style brass lamp, a telephone, large Apple iMac, MacBook Pro, iPad, and an iPhone. Seemed someone went a little crazy at the Apple Store. There was also two back-up drives and about a dozen jump drives. This was definitely the big leagues.

Behind the desk, was a white lacquered credenza with a huge arrangement of white lilies, art books, candles, a black tray with mineral and flat water, napkins with the company logo, jars of mixed nuts, pretzels, and black and white M&Ms. In the corner, was a small black velvet settee with black and white striped pillows like the chairs. Also, a small brass and glass coffee table with a stack of art books, a small arrangement of white roses, a very modern brass floor lamp, and a black and white geometric print rug.

The office was beautiful and unlike any of the ones downstairs. I looked around and thought how cool it would be to work in this space permanently. I sat down in one of the chairs facing the desk and waited for someone to appear.

Ten minutes later, the phone rang. I looked around and no one appeared, and the phone stopped ringing. A few minutes later it rang again, so I answered it. "Hello, Morgan Grant." I didn't know whose office it was so I played it safe. I knew I could always transfer the call to the right department.

"Great, you're there. I need you to familiarize yourself with the leases for the D.C., Atlanta, Charlotte, and Dallas offices. Also, get the number of employees. I need to know if there are any open positions, and if so, how many. Call Estella in Human Resources and tell her what you need. Then, make a list of the top three commercial real estate brokers in London and Paris."

He was speaking so quickly, I never got a chance to tell him that whoever he was trying to reach wasn't there. I put the call on speaker, got my phone and recorded everything he was saying while jotting down whatever I could catch. I wanted to make sure I relayed the information correctly to whomever the office belonged to.

"Then go to Brockman's, ask for Cameron and pick up the things he has for me. Tony will pick you up tomorrow and bring you to the airport."

"When the assistant arrives, who should I say called?"

"Phillippe. Don't tell me I just gave all that to the receptionist. Human Resources said my assistant was in her office."

"I'm sorry, but no one was here when I arrived. I'm waiting on someone to give me instructions for my next assignment."

"What did Human Resources tell you?"

"There was an emergency. Then I was handed a card with this office number and told to report here for my next assignment."

He sighed. "Are you Gabriella Townsend?"

"Yes."

"I'm Phillippe Marchant, you'll be working with me."

"For how long?"

"Excuse me?"

"Usually, when I start an assignment, I'm also told the duration."

"This isn't a temp job. You've been hired to work with me."

"Oh, I didn't..."

"It's not your fault. I'll deal with Human Resources. I'm in Seattle putting out a fire. I'll see you tomorrow." Click.

I pressed the STOP button on my phone recorder and looked around *my office*. All my hard work and patience had paid off. I jumped up and down doing the happy dance in *my office*. I walked over and sat on my settee, my chairs and touched everything in *my office*.

I finally sat down in the odd desk chair and sighed. This is perfect. It's decorated exactly how I would have done it. "Wow, thank you God." I collected myself and got to work.

Just as I was about to head out to Brockman's, my phone rang. I picked it up and answered, "Phillippe Marchant's office."

"Gabriella."

Now that I know this is my office, I took the time to

really listen to his voice. It was deep and sounded like smooth port wine. "Yes, sir."

"First of all, it's Phillippe."

"Yes, sir. I mean Phillippe."

"Call James Marshall's office. His number is in the Contacts on your computer. Let them know we'll be attending the gala and that I'll give James the check when I meet with him."

"Is there anyone else I need to inform about the party?"

"Excuse me?"

"You said *us*."

"Crap. Is there a black folder on your desk?"

"No."

"Go into my office and look on my desk."

"Hold on."

I walked over to the sliding wood door across from my desk, and pulled it back. My mouth dropped open again for the second time today. In the almost two years I've worked here, I've never seen an office like this one. It's not an office, but a loft. The very masculine scent greeted me at the door… tobacco, musk, leather and something spicy I can't name.

The walls were the same color black as the ones in my office, but in a flat finish. In the far left corner was a lounge area with a large black leather sofa, a couple of oversized brown leather club chairs, and a large square distressed wood coffee table with a large art book opened to a page on vintage cars. To the left of the door were shiny black bookcases filled with books, albums and a vintage record player.

In the other corner, was a large rectangular dark wood table with eight square black leather and brass chairs around it. Above the table, was a cool vintage light fixture expanding the length of the table. An antique brass open shelving unit was on the wall facing the conference table. On the wall above the shelving unit was a large, round mirror. An incredible plaster and iron sculpture sat on top of the shelving unit.

I stepped inside and the view of San Francisco took my breath away. The wall facing the conference table was floor to ceiling windows...a billionaire's view. I looked around and finally cast my attention on the large, sleek and shiny black lacquered desk. It looked more like art than a desk. The only things on it were a large Apple iMac, a telephone, a couple of black lacquer trays, and a small tray filled with black Montblanc pens and black old school pencils. The chair seemed out of place in front of the desk. It was black velvet, with a feminine shape to it.

It was clear Phillippe was an art lover. There were interesting pieces accessorizing the space. The large black and white print on the wall behind the desk was my favorite...a pair of hands. It was simple and dramatic. Instead of a light cluttering the desk, there was a cool, bubble bulb chandelier hanging over the desk. Behind the desk was a black vintage credenza with a tray of bottled water, glasses, napkins and three glass canisters...one with mixed nuts, one with black and white M&Ms and one with pretzels. I see Mr. Marchant likes to snack, which explains the identical set up in my office.

I walked up to the desk and inside one of the trays was a black folder with "Gabriella" written on it. I picked up the folder and went back to my office.

"I have it."

"Do you see an itinerary?"

I opened the folder and thumbed through the pages searching for the document. "No."

"Crap! I'm sorry. This thing in Seattle caught me off guard. You and I will be visiting the offices I asked you to get information on before coming home. After a brief break, we'll be heading to London and Paris to look for new office space. We have to attend the Marshall Pediatrics Spring Gala while we're in Charlotte. I apologize for throwing all of this on you at the last minute. Do you need a couple of extra hours to get packed?"

Couple of hours? How about a couple of days! The last time I had on an evening gown, was the prom. "That would help."

"If you need a dress, when you go to Brockman's tell Cameron I said to fix you up with whatever you need."

"That won't be necessary."

"I insist. Consider it my way of apologizing for the crazy first day."

"Thank you."

"I'll see you tomorrow at three."

"Bye."

phillippe

She probably thinks I'm the worst boss in the world. I hope she doesn't regret working with me. Truth is, when I read her resume, I was very impressed and didn't need to meet with her. Anyone with her intelligence willing to work as a floater until something becomes available, understands what it means to work here. She has the kind of loyalty I want on my team.

Tony's security check didn't turn up anything for me to be concerned about which pleased me even more. I would, however, have preferred someone a couple of years older, but her dedication to the company convinced me to give her a chance.

I hope she likes her office. I worked closely with my decorator to make sure it was filled with things she liked. Tony is thorough in his research. How he found out her favorite colors was beyond me. It was perfect that we have very similar tastes, because it makes for a cohesive work environment. Her love of art was one of the other reasons I hired her. We'll be doing a lot of traveling and I like visiting museums and art galleries. It will be nice to have someone I can share that with.

First things first, I've got to get this company healthy.

chapter two

gabriella

I WENT TO BROCKMAN'S AND met Cameron, my new best friend. He informed me my new boss is a wonderful man with impeccable taste. Phillippe failed to mention that the bags I was picking up were two black Gucci duffles and a matching garment bag filled with things for our trip. Apparently, there's no time for him to go home before we leave.

The gowns Cameron pulled were incredible. Sure, Phillippe told me the dress was his way of apologizing, but he really hadn't done anything worth that gorgeous fuchsia jersey Donna Karan that fit me like a glove.

When I tried to object, Cameron insisted. He said, "Mr. Marchant told me to take care of you and not to let you leave without something you loved. He said he needs you to feel confident, because it's an important event for Morgan Grant."

After hearing that statement, I shut up and let him work his magic. I had a beautiful evening gown and accessories when he finished. To celebrate my new job, I treated myself to a couple of things off the sale rack…a simple black DVF wrap dress and a black Theory pants suit. I told Cameron I needed to save up for the black Donna Karan suit, but it sure looked good on me.

After I spoke with Phillippe the first time, I called my mother and told her about my new job. When he called again about my traveling with him, I called her back. Once she stopped screaming, she said, "I'll get my suitcases."

It was eight thirty when I got home and I still had to pack. I opened the front door and walked inside with my arms full. "Mom," I called out. No answer. "Mom," I called again.

"I'm in your room."

I went upstairs and on my bed were two of my mom's suitcases. One was filled with my lingerie and a pharmacy of toiletries. "What's going on?"

"I picked up a few necessities and packed your good lingerie. I also got you a new robe, pajamas and slippers. What's that?" she said, pointing to the bags.

"I bought a dress and a suit."

"And the long garment bag?" She walked over and unzipped the bag. "Oh Gabby, this is beautiful." She looked at the label. "Donna Karan. Why did you buy an evening gown?"

"I didn't. My boss did. Besides, it's for work."

"Tell me more about this job and Phillippe Marchant. I couldn't find any pictures of him on the internet. It's like he's a ghost."

I continued packing as I answered her question. "He's new with the company and this trip has to do with some of the corporate building leases."

"I see. Is he single or married?"

"I don't know, and how is that relevant to my job?"

"What exactly are you going to be doing?"

"The usual Assistant duties."

"Since when did wearing an expensive evening gown and international travel become *usual* Assistant duties?"

"We have to attend a charity gala as representatives of Morgan Grant." Now wasn't the best time to tell her I've yet to meet my new boss. Nor was it a wise thing to let her know my internet search wasn't any better than hers.

"Uh-huh…you sure that's all?"

"What's that supposed to mean?"

"It sounds like he may have hired you for…" She raised an eyebrow. "You know…"

"What mom?"

"Baby, you're a very intelligent young woman, but when it comes to men, especially men who are…just make sure one of your *duties* isn't to be his bed buddy."

"Mom!"

"Don't look so surprised. Your mom knows a few things." She winked and started towards the door. "I'd better hear from you at least twice a day."

"Yes ma'am."

"I'll make you something to eat. What time are you leaving?"

"Tony is picking me up at two."

She stopped walking and turned around. "Who's Tony?"

"The driver."

"The driver? Uh-huh, you do know I'll be here when you leave?"

"Mom, it's my job. Will it make you feel better if I have you on speaker phone the entire ride to the airport?" I teased.

"Yes."

"Mom…really?"

∞ ⸲⸺ ∞ ⸲⸺ ∞ ⸲⸺ ∞

It was very late when I crawled into bed. I was exhausted and not sure if there'd be a chance for sleep on the flight. When I woke up at ten thirty, I brushed my teeth and headed down to the kitchen. I came around the corner and saw my mom sitting at the table. I coughed and she looked up. "Morning sunshine. What time did you finally go to sleep?"

"Four."

"Want some coffee?"

"Yes, please." I sat down and she placed a large white mug in front of me and kissed me on the forehead. After the first sip, I let out a deep sigh. "That's good."

"How about some eggs and toast?"

"Please. Thank you." After breakfast, she helped me finish packing. I looked at the clock and it was one, and I needed to get dressed.

At one forty-five, the doorbell rang. I opened the door and swallowed. Standing in front of me was a bald, dark chocolate human wall with a beard, wearing a black suit. I swallowed hard and looked at my mother. She cocked her head and folded her arms in front of her chest. I knew that meant she'd be in the car behind me all the way to the airport.

I let Tony in and showed him where the bags were. It took him a couple of trips to load everything into the car. When he returned, he asked, "Are you ready?"

"Excuse me," my mother jumped in, and Tony looked at her. "Exactly who are you?"

"I'm Mr. Marchant's driver." Tony looked more like his muscle.

"Is that all?" My mother's follow up question.

"Yes. Miss Townsend, we need to leave."

I hugged my mother. "Have a safe trip…call me."

"I will."

"Love you, baby."

"Love you, mom."

phillippe

I took this job with the understanding that I had the full support of the board and the senior management. Now, I find out, that's not true. The Senior Vice President of Facilities failed to inform me about the situation in Seattle. This whole thing has made me a little leery about the validity of his report.

Now on top of everything else I have to deal with, I have to relocate an office. How is it possible no one knew what was going on with that building?

This situation is just another example of how out of date the operations are. If the upper management had been communicating with each other, I'm sure someone would have picked up on the problem.

I'm grateful I was able to buy some time with the

new owner. It meant forfeiting the lease buyout money, but I can live with that. What I couldn't live with was the twenty million in lost revenue if the facility had to shut down. I'm not exactly pleased with the temporary location, but that's why it's temporary. At least I can get everything moved and only lose about three million.

The main reason I'm taking this road trip is because I don't trust the Facilities report I was given. I need to meet with the Vice President of Operations in each of these offices and find out what they know. I cannot afford a repeat of the Seattle situation right now.

I have a branch relocation plan, but I didn't want to implement it for at least a year…six months, if pushed. I want to fire the current Senior Vice President of Facilities, but that would leave me without anyone in that position. At this point, I've got to play the hand I've been dealt.

I contacted a headhunter and had her submit a list of potential replacements for my lazy ass Senior Vice President of Facilities. Once Tony checks them out, I'll start interviewing. My ideal candidate for a short term fix is Gabriella, but she's not ready. I'd send Tony, but I need his help on this road trip. I have a feeling Seattle wasn't the only office with a circumspect lease. Seems I'm stuck with this idiot for a little longer.

I forgot to send Gabriella a picture of Tony. On first glance, he looks intimidating, but that's what I need. We go way back. When I took this position, I insisted he be added to my team. He's more like my assistant. He knows how I work and has a vast knowledge of commercial real estate and construction. He's also in charge of my security. Before I do business with or hire anyone, he runs a thorough background check.

When I agreed to take this job, he began gathering

information on all the board members and senior executives. I needed to know who would be loyal to me. At the present, the team consists of three people...me, Tony and Gabriella.

chapter three

gabriella

WE PULLED UP NEXT TO a huge jet and parked. My nerves were on edge. I should have known we'd be traveling on the company jet. Tony got out and opened my door. "Mr. Marchant will be here shortly."

"Thank you." He helped me out of the car and my mind filled with a thousand possible ways this could be bad. I walked up the stairs and when I crossed the threshold of the plane, my mouth dropped open. I looked around the beautiful space and figured if I were being sold into white slavery, at least I was going in style with a great dress.

"Good afternoon Miss Townsend. I'm Gil." Oh great another strange man. Am I the only female working for this man?

"Hello." I shook the gentleman's hand.

"Can I get you something while we wait for Mr. Marchant?"

Alcohol wasn't an option, I needed to stay alert. "A mineral water please. Thank you."

"Have a seat and I'll be right back."

I sat down and watched as Tony loaded the bags, then disappeared. I closed my eyes and said a little prayer, followed by a couple of deep breaths. Then I sent a text to my mother, *"So far so good."*

Gil returned. "Here you are Miss." He looked out the window. "Mr. Marchant has arrived."

My heart leapt into my throat. I took a long sip from my glass, popped a breath mint, and stood up. I brushed the imaginary lint off my sleeve, rubbed my tongue across my teeth checking for lipstick, and folded my hands in front of me. I looked out the window hoping to get a glimpse of the elusive Phillippe Marchant as he got out of the black Bentley, but Tony "The Wall," was blocking my view.

I held my breath and aimed my eyes at the entrance, but all I saw was his back, followed by the voice from the phone.

"Tony, make sure Marcos knows to go to my place and check on things. Have him forward anything that looks important to the D.C. office, and I'll see you on board."

Now I was confused. I thought Tony was the driver. Who the crap is Marcos? I'm surrounded by strange men. I looked down briefly. When I raised my head, my eyes landed on a very tall, young, hot man walking towards me. My body reacted in a way I had never experienced. I was trembling from head to toe, and a strange sensation settled in the lower half of my body.

I've never seen an executive or man that looked like

this. Most of the executives at Morgan Grant were older and definitely not this fine. This man's skin looked like rich black coffee. I wanted to touch his face to see if it felt as smooth as it looked. He was wearing a light grey suit and a simple white shirt, with the first few buttons undone to reveal more of that beautiful dark skin. He continued toward me and his spicy scent filled up the plane. This couldn't be…

"Phillippe, we finally meet." He extended his hand and I saw his guns. My God, every muscle in his body was at attention and now he was giving me permission to touch him.

"Hello." I shook his hand and a spark erupted. No really, an electric shock.

"Must be the carpet," he joked.

"Sir," Gil appeared.

"Gil, thank you for taking care of Miss Townsend. Once we get on our way, please serve lunch. I haven't eaten since this morning. When Tony gets back, tell the pilot wheels up. Thank you."

"Yes sir." Gil disappeared to the rear of the plane.

"Gabriella," he looked at me and the most salacious thought crossed my mind. For a moment, I forgot I was a good girl excited about this amazing job God had blessed me with. "Have a seat. We have a lot to discuss before we land."

I smiled, sat down, grabbed the necessary files, and buckled my seat belt. I reached for my iPad and when I straightened up, Phillippe was sitting across from me. He had taken his jacket off, revealing more of his incredible build. He removed his cufflinks and began rolling up his shirt sleeves. I was fascinated by the crisp white cotton bending at his will, releasing more of his demanding, intoxicating scent. I tried to focus on my iPad, telling myself, *Don't look at him. If you do, you might suffer the same fate as Lot's wife and turn into a pillar of salt.* I lifted up my iPad and pretended to read. All of a sudden the plane seemed dark. I looked up and Tony was walking towards us.

"I told the pilot we're ready," he said to Phillippe.

"Let Gil know, and ask him to bring me a glass of ice water. Thank you." He looked at me and I was grateful to be sitting because every muscle in my body was numb. "Turn your iPad off until after take off." He capped off his comment with a smile. Dimples. Are you kidding me?

His looks are strong and commanding until he smiles and then he becomes a real life sex fantasy. His eyes look like black diamonds, and those have got to be the whitest teeth I've ever seen.

What is wrong with me? He's not even my type. Like I have a type. My last relationship was with Todd Elliot, my lab partner. Even then, I think it was a pity thing on both our parts. He was short, fair skinned, sweaty palms and every time he kissed me, it felt like I was being kissed by a fish.

I looked at Phillippe's lips and wondered how those, gorgeous full lips would feel pressed against mine. I bet they're soft. He probably doesn't kiss like a fish, but like a man who knows how to take charge. His kisses are probably filled with a lot of passion. I bit my lower lip, lost in my fantasy of kissing him.

"Gabriella…Gabriella…"

"I'm sorry. I forgot my mother asked me to text her before we took off."

"Please do, I understand mothers."

Please don't be a mama's boy. That would be a shame, not to mention what it would do to my fantasy. I texted mama, *"I'm okay. He's really nice. We're headed to D.C. Will text when we land. Talk to you later. Love, Gabby."*

THE GOOD GIRL

"Be careful. Love you, baby."

About an hour into our flight, Gil appeared with lunch. I tried to focus on work, but it was difficult with Phillippe sitting across from me. He even eats sexy.

He wiped his mouth. "I'm sure you have questions."

Yes, I do. Why is Tony traveling with us? Why was it necessary for me to come on this trip? Not that I'm complaining, but with the work I'm doing, I could have stayed at the office. "How did you come to work for Morgan Grant?"

He looked at Tony and then back at me. "Uhm, the Chairman and I were at a social function and started talking. I made a great impression, a lucrative offer was made and I accepted." I heard Tony cough. "Why did you want to work at Morgan Grant?"

"They showed the most opportunity for growth."

"What's your favorite department?"

"It was Mergers and Acquisitions, until I spent some time in Advertising."

"What changed your mind?"

"I like the creative energy."

"I see." He smiled. "This definitely isn't advertising, but there is a little creativity involved."

"What do you do exactly?"

He shifted in his seat and sipped his coffee. "Let's just say, we'll be doing a little bit of everything."

"Like going to charity events?" I smiled.

"Exactly. Did Cameron help you with a dress?"

"Yes, but I think it's too…"

"Nonsense. You will probably need to add a few more to your wardrobe, so when we get back…"

Is he kidding? Unless he's going to buy me a dress every time I need one, we need to talk about my salary. "I don't…"

"Is there a problem?"

"I can't afford to buy dresses like the one you bought. I'll do my best, but…I'm not complaining about my salary, because the standard Executive Assistant salary is way better than…"

"What are you talking about?"

"I assumed I was hired to be your Executive Assistant."

"I know I've had a lot on my mind the past few days, but when I confirmed your position with Human Resources, I was very clear about your salary. I felt based on your experience and the job duties, you deserved a little more." He scrolled down his email and forwarded me a copy. "See for yourself."

When I opened the email, I tried not to show my excitement. Instead, I saw myself in the black Donna Karan suit plus a new pair of shoes.

"I'm sorry about the mix up. This thing with the Seattle office has had us all a little distracted."

"I understand." I looked up and that smile sent a jolt straight to my core.

"Do you like your office?"

I shifted in my seat. "It's beautiful. How did you know my favorite color?"

"Which one?" Tony coughed and Phillippe cut him a look.

"Black, I love it."

"I wanted the spaces to complement each other. I like black as well."

"Your office is…wow. It's a cool place to work." I'll never tell him, that it looks like a cool rich boy bachelor pad. I already see myself ordering pizza and hot wings for him and his friends on fight night or during the basketball playoffs. He probably has four televisions so he can watch multiple games at the same time.

"Thank you. I apologize about the desk chair."

"The desk chair?" Thank God he brought it up, because that's the only thing I don't like about my office.

"I thought it best if you picked it out yourself, as well as your dictation chair in front of my desk." It's very sweet that he wants me to select my *dictation chair* for his office.

"Thank you. What about the chair that's there?"

"The decorator...I don't like it, but if you do...oh, the television should be installed by the time we get back, as well as the print. There was a crack in the frame and it had to be redone."

"Television?" I really don't see where that's necessary, but I'm not going to complain.

"We'll be working late and I thought it would be a nice treat."

"Thank you."

"Feel free to add pictures and anything else to make the space comfortable."

"Thank you." It was all a little overwhelming.

"You need to hire a receptionist. There's a temp in place now, but we need someone permanent. Human Resources will be sending you some options. Select three and give their names to Tony. Once he's checked them out, you can interview them."

The past twenty-four hours seemed like a dream. Not only did I have a fabulous new job, my own office, a hot boss, and from the sound of it, I'm about to hire my first employee. Thank you God, this is great.

I tried to stifle my yawns, but I was exhausted. I kept hoping Phillippe would take a nap so I could as well. Unfortunately, he had a long list of things he wanted to discuss. When I went to the restroom, I spotted Tony in one of the chairs asleep. I envied him.

phillippe

I tried not to stare at her, but I'm shocked at how beautiful she is. Nowhere in Tony's report did he mention how beautiful Gabriella is. My last assistant was a pretty woman in her mid sixties. Mrs. Reynolds was more like a mother. However, this woman sitting across from me is a lustful distraction. I'm not sure if this is going to work.

I tried to play off that spark thing, but it was real. Nothing like that has ever happened to me, not even with Chantal.

I'm trying not to stare at her, but those are the sexiest lips I've ever seen. Full and juicy. I could watch her talk all day. I wonder how she kisses. Did I just say that? What is wrong with me? She's not even my type. But her petite frame and those curves are doing something to me. I wonder how her hair looks straight. The curls framing her face make her look sweet and innocent, but those lips…maybe I should send her home and just communicate via the phone and a few video chats. Who am I kidding? That wouldn't help, because even talking to her on the phone, her face would be in my head and I'd be envisioning those lips.

When I sat down across from her, I was glad she couldn't see how my body was reacting to being so close to her. How am I going to spend the next month or so on the road with her?

"Turn your iPad off until after take off." When she looked up at me with those big brown eyes, I was done. I polished off that glass of ice water in one swallow and it didn't seem like the air was working.

I was exhausted and planned to sleep, but when I saw

her, that plan instantly went up in flames. I didn't want to miss one moment being in her presence.

What is that parfum she's wearing? It's taken over the plane. When I wiped my mouth with my napkin, her scent was there. It's like spicy vanilla and tobacco, unusual for a woman, but very seductive. I've never been around a woman as mesmerizing as she is.

"Were you able to reach your mother?" I asked. Maybe hearing her talk about her mother will kill the lustful thoughts I'm having.

"Yes. I promised I'd call when we land."

No such luck. The sweet sound of her voice traveled into my ear and danced around my head before journeying to my core, awakening something I assumed had become immune to sweet talk. The funny thing is, she didn't say anything seductive or enticing. It's just something about her. I can't quite put my hand on it, although I wouldn't mind touching every inch of her.

After we reached cruising level, Gil served lunch. I was starving. I drank so much coffee in Seattle, I think if you cut me, I'll bleed Sumatra roast coffee.

So far the only thing that matches up to the report Tony gave me, is that she's very smart. Considering the amount of time she had to gather the information I requested, she did very well. I'm convinced she'll be able to handle any task I assign her.

She caught me off guard with her question. She's a lot more perceptive than I anticipated, which is what she'll need working with clients and the other executives. However, I've got to be careful not to slip up and make her suspicious of me. I need to keep the truth about her job and my position a secret as long as I can. I want her to be fully trained and comfortable working with me and Tony, before telling her why I really hired her. The longer she believes she was hired to be the Assistant to the new President, the better. She needs to believe there's someone I report to.

If Tony were awake, I could ask him about his report on Gabriella and the obvious missing facts. At the top of the list, why didn't he disclose how beautiful she is. It's as if he thought I wouldn't want to hire her because I had other intentions for her. I've gotta say, he wouldn't be too far off base.

When it comes to a receptionist, it had better be an older, married woman.

chapter four

gabriella

WORKING WITH PHILLIPPE HAS BEEN way more than I expected. Turns out, the problem in Seattle was with the building. It had been sold and the new owner wasn't renewing any of the leases. Instead, they bought out all the leases and gave the tenants one month to vacate. Because Morgan Grant housed half of the building, Phillippe managed to negotiate some extra time, until the temporary space is ready.

We went in and evaluated the current and future needs of Morgan Grant and the other tenants. Then we looked at other possible locations. My job was to compare the cost to buy the buildings in each of the cities we visited, and take over all the leases verses just relocating Morgan Grant to another property. I took all the data, compiled my report, and presented it to Phillippe.

This was how the first three weeks went.

We finally made it to Charlotte and all three of us were exhausted. Phillippe checked us into our hotel rooms with strict orders to eat and sleep.

The following morning we all met in Phillippe's suite for breakfast. The moment Tony opened the door, the aroma of fresh brewed coffee greeted me.

"Good morning Miss Townsend."

He still won't smile, but at least he's not giving me intimidating looks anymore. "Good morning Tony."

I was beginning to relax in my job, in spite of the crush on my boss. Maybe it was his intelligence, or the way he took charge in meetings, or his sense of humor. Who am I kidding? It's the whole package. If I were to tell God exactly what kind of man I want, it would be one like Phillippe. A man who knows how to handle his business. Who's gentle and strong. Who makes me laugh, loves art and isn't afraid to admit when he's made a mistake. Let's face it, if he looks like he just stepped off the cover of a romance novel, that's even better.

I followed the aroma and found Phillippe standing at the window on the phone. He had his back to me and the sight of his broad shoulders and tight backside, did more for waking me up than the coffee.

"I understand you don't like this, but…I see…I don't think that's a good idea…uh-huh…uh-huh…no…if we do that, it could set us back at least six months…I don't agree…the whole thing could have been avoided if he'd told someone… exactly…a million three…about three million…exactly…I'm already on it…a couple of weeks, maybe longer…no…okay."

I walked over to the buffet and started piling food on a

plate while staring at Phillippe. My, my, my…God, You have incredible sculpting skills. I wonder what he looks like naked.

He started pacing, then looked up, saw me and smiled. I quickly turned my attention to my overloaded plate and put the serving spoon down.

"We'll continue this when I get back…not yet…because it's too soon…yes it is…I do, but not now…I'll let you know…no…don't you trust me?…thank you…bye." He pressed the button ending the call and placed his phone on the table. He rubbed his head with his hands and exhaled. Clearly whoever he was speaking with, upset him. A few seconds later, he seemed calm. "Good morning Gabriella. How did you sleep?"

"Well. Thank you. And yourself?"

He hesitated with his answer. "I slept." He walked over to the buffet and picked up a plate. "Tell me about your family."

"My family?"

"Yes. Tony said he met your mother when he picked you up."

He returned to the table with a modest serving of scrambled eggs, bacon and asparagus. He sat down in the chair across from me and looked at my plate. Oh great, he probably thinks I'm a drooling idiot and a greedy pig.

"My dad's a lawyer and my mother is a teacher."

He nodded as he chewed and swallowed. "Any siblings?"

"A younger brother. He's a junior at MIT."

"Impressive. What does he want to do?"

"I'm not quite sure. He says he feels God is leading him into research. He's only eighteen and works harder than I do."

"Wow. We may need to hire him." He smiled and refilled his coffee cup. "What grade does your mother teach?"

He sipped his coffee. His dark full lips looked even more delicious holding the white cup prisoner as he turned it up.

"She's an étiquette teacher."

"Really?"

"Actually, she teaches protocol to executives." He looked vexed. "When my dad went to China, he asked her to help him not embarrass himself. She researched the culture and learned how he should conduct himself in business and social situations. He made a great impression and it helped with his negotiations. When one of his friends was preparing to go, he asked my dad for help and my mother coached him. He hired her and her business was born."

"I might need to hire your mother." He sipped his coffee. "What do you do in your free time? Any hobbies?"

"I like visiting art galleries and the museum. Once a month I take some of the kids from my church to the museum. And, I teach Sunday School." It was difficult concentrating on my answers with him staring at me.

He smiled. "How old are the kids in your Sunday School class?"

"Eight."

"Do you have a boyfriend?" He picked up a stalk of asparagus, bit down and my stomach danced.

I cleared my throat. "Uhm, no." This is sheer torture. I should have just ordered room service and came over after I finished eating. Sitting here answering personal questions and watching his lips…it is way too early for…

"No? You've got to be kidding?" He smiled.

"No. I guess I've been too focused on getting stable in my career." That was a lie. There was no one because there was no one who interested me, or found me interesting. "What about you…married?"

He almost choked and patted his chest. "No, I'm not married." He sipped his water and smiled.

"Is there a girlfriend or girlfriends I need to know about?"

"Excuse me?"

"Is there someone whose calls you always answer, or who I'll need to rearrange your schedule for?" I smiled.

"There was someone, but it ended recently."

"I didn't mean to…"

"You didn't…we just wanted different things."

"How long were you together?"

"Three years." He sipped his coffee and carefully placed the white china cup back on the saucer and wiped his mouth.

"So if some chick calls or shows up and says she's your girlfriend, I'll call Tony and have him take care of her." I smiled at Tony and he gave me a thumbs up.

"Funny."

"What about you, what's your family like?"

"My family…my mother is an American who fell in love with a handsome African Frenchman. That's how she tells the story."

"Wow." I nodded. "How does he tell the story?"

"His version wasn't as romantic. He said it was her hips and laugh that put a spell on him."

I smiled. "Very romantic." He nodded and the corner of his mouth turned up slightly. "How long have they been married?"

"They were married twenty-nine years." He shifted in his seat. "He died three years ago."

"I'm sorry." I wanted to walk over and wrap my arms around him.

"Thank you."

"That explains your name."

"Yes, I was named after my grandfather. My grandfather was French and my grandmother was African."

"Wow."

phillippe

I didn't think the company was in such bad shape when I agreed to take over. This antiquated dinosaur is in need of a major overhaul. I know the changes I've proposed to the board are drastic, but if I don't force some action now, there won't be a company to save.

If I had the support I was told I'd have, things would be a lot different and this transition, much easier. I am not happy about being on the road for extended periods but, until I build a trustworthy team, I've got no choice. The only highlight to this insane travel schedule is spending time with Gabriella.

I can't believe she doesn't have a boyfriend. How is that even possible? She's an amazing girl…smart, funny, sweet and beautiful. I enjoy talking with her.

I almost choked when she asked if I was married or had a girlfriend. I don't know what Chantal and I were. Towards the end, it seemed like we spent more time fighting than anything else. I think if she'd been a little more supportive, we could have worked out all our problems. The number one reason we broke up was her not understanding why I had to take this job.

I understand Morgan Grant, and I know I can bring it back to the kind of company it was. To an outsider, it seems like everything is fine. The reality is, there's a lot of debt, dead weight, and antiquated operations and policies. Once I get the company healthy, I plan to get myself healthy. I want what my parents had, a loving marriage and lots of children.

I don't think I shared that story about my parents with any of my former girlfriends. Watching the gentleness on Gabriella's face as I shared the tidbit was refreshing. If I'd shared that with Chantal, she would have thought I was weak. Being in love or surrendering to love doesn't make you weak, it makes you strong and smart.

I looked at Gabriella and still couldn't believe there wasn't a man that saw what I saw. She's the complete package. When we get to Europe I'm going to arrange some private museum tours. I think she'll like that.

chapter five

gabriella

PHILLIPPE TOLD ME TO TAKE the day to rest and get ready for the party. He said if I needed help with my hair and makeup to go to the hotel salon and charge it to his suite. I could have taken his offer a couple of ways. One, he didn't like my hair and makeup or, that he wanted me to amp it up.

I don't wear a lot of makeup every day, but I do know how to kick it up when I have to. Besides, when Cameron helped me with the gown, he suggested I do a complimentary pink lip, black liner and falsies. I'm already having a problem being relaxed in this dress and heels. I don't think I can handle false eyelashes as well.

I looked in the mirror and almost didn't recognize

myself. The salon did a good job with my hair. I have to let Cameron know the makeup was right on point.

I sent my mother a selfie of me all dolled up. *"What do you think?"*

"You look beautiful. Daddy says he likes your hair. Have fun. Call me later."

My phone dinged with a message from Phillippe. *"Gabriella, meet me in the lobby."*

I took a deep breath, grabbed my wrap and bag, and headed for the elevator. When I got to the lobby, I didn't see Tony or Phillippe. I stood close to the entrance with my eyes on the elevators. A few minutes later, Tony walked past me.

"Tony." He stopped and turned around.

"Miss Townsend?" His eyes were wide and he smiled. "Wow."

"Phillippe told me to meet him in the lobby."

"He's in the bar."

"I'll get him and we'll meet you at the car." He turned and left.

I took a deep breath and went to the bar. I looked around and saw Phillippe standing at the end of the bar looking at the television. My heart skyrocketed to my throat. He looked like the black James Bond...suave, classy, sexy, dangerous. I walked over and tapped him on the arm and it was like tapping steel.

He turned slightly and smiled, then frowned. Oh crap, I made a mistake with the hair, or maybe the dress. Cameron assured me this was how Phillippe wanted me to look. He stepped back and his smile reappeared. "Gigi?"

"Excuse me?"

"I'm sorry. Gabriella. You look..." He slowly looked me up and down. I felt flattered and pretty.

"Tony's out front with the car." I walked out of the bar ahead of him and felt his eyes on me.

My nerves were racing around my stomach at the thought of possibly dancing with Phillippe. I kept telling myself, this is a work function, not a date. So what if that means spending a little time pressed up against my hot boss with his large, strong hands holding me, then so be it.

"Tony did you see how beautiful Gabriella looks?"

"Yes." He looked at me via the rearview mirror. "Like the hair."

"Thank you." Phillippe kept staring at me. "Is there anything I need to know?" He didn't say anything. I repeated my question. "Phillippe, is there anything I need to know?"

He cleared his throat and shifted in his seat. "Uhm… no, I'll introduce you to James and his wife and then just follow my lead."

"Okay."

"We're representing Morgan Grant, but it's also a party, so I want you to have a good time." He smiled.

Since I began working with Phillippe, this was the first time I'd seen him at a loss for words.

We pulled up to valet parking and Phillippe got out, walked around, and helped me out of the car. He took my arm and wrapped it around his bent elbow. "You have nothing to be nervous about," he assured me.

"What about Tony?"

"He'll join us after he takes care of the car."

We continued inside and it wasn't what I expected. Instead of a stuffy dinner, it was a carnival. There were game booths around the walls of the ball room, clowns, stilt walkers, balloon artists and gourmet carnival food. The theme was perfect for a children's charity.

THE GOOD GIRL

"Wow." I was relieved, but I was also disappointed about not being wrapped in Phillippe's strong arms dancing.

"This is so different from last year."

"Excuse me?"

"Last year it was a dinner and dancing." He looked around and a huge smile appeared on his face. "So what do you want to play first?"

I looked around the colorfully decorated ballroom. It reminded me of my family trips to the fair and my dad playing ring toss so he could win me a giant teddy bear. It took him four years, but he finally did it. "Ring toss."

"Are you kidding?"

I looked at him. "With your height, we should be able to do some damage."

"Okay, ring toss it is."

We headed over to the ring toss game. Phillippe took his jacket off and handed it to me. "Okay, so what are we taking home?"

I looked at the prizes and spotted what I wanted. "The bear."

He looked at me. "Are you kidding? That thing is huge. How are you going to get it home?"

"You have a plane." I smiled.

"How many rings does it take to win the bear?" he asked the attendant.

"Get one on the red bottle."

"The red bottle?" Phillippe strained to find the red bottle.

"Yep." The attendant pointed to the red bottle deep in the middle of the green bottles.

"I see."

"Get a ring on it and the little lady takes the bear of her choice home."

He looked at me. "You sure about this?"

"Yep."

phillippe

When I called Cameron and told him to take care of Gabriella, I had no idea this is what he was going to do. I was already having a problem being around her and to see her like this… she's gorgeous. The way that dress hugs her curves is… and her hair. I like the curls, but straight, cascading down her back is very sexy.

I was doing fine until I saw her thigh. When she climbed into the car, that deep split revealed a beautiful thick, smooth, caramel colored thigh. I've always been a leg man, with my taste veering more to the long legs of models, not those of petite, curvy women.

I walked around the car, grateful for the breeze, because this woman was doing things to me I hadn't expected. I got into the backseat and sat a respectable distance from her, still staring at her legs. She crossed her legs and although she covered them with her wrap my mind wandered. I imagined how both of those gorgeous thick thighs would feel wrapped around my hips as we…oh my God. I tried to push the thought out, but I couldn't.

My collar and tie felt tight. I needed some air. I rolled the window down and inhaled the cool air. I managed to compose myself and pay her a compliment. "Tony, did you see how beautiful Gabriella looks?" I didn't hear Tony's reply, because I was focused on her.

It took a moment for it to register that she was talking

to me. Her voice no longer sounded sweet and demure. In my mind it was sexy and seductive. With the help of a flat iron and an expensive gown, Gabriella went from being my sweet, young assistant to a sexy woman I wanted in my bed.

My mind was full of thoughts no good girl should know anything about...like how she would feel lying underneath me...how her skin tastes...how her voice will sound when I hit that sweet spot...how her breasts will feel in my hands...what is wrong with me? She's not my type and she's too young. But being around her just feels right.

I would have paid any amount of money that man asked for that bear. The look on her face when that ring landed on the red bottle was worth the five hundred dollars it cost me. I don't know what came over me, or why I picked her up and spun her around. Why did she have to look up at me with those beautiful dark brown eyes and pouty lips, begging me to kiss her? I was about to answer her silent request, when we were interrupted.

"Sir, which bear, the one with the blue ribbon or the red bandana?"

I cleared my throat. "It's up to her." She handed me my jacket.

"I'll take the red one. Thank you."

"Would you like to try for another one?" he asked as he handed me the bear.

"I think he needs to give his arm a rest." She smiled and winked.

I looked around the room and spotted Tony at the dart booth. "There's Tony. Maybe you can convince him to win a friend for your bear." She looked in the direction I was pointing and back at me with those eyes.

"I see the perfect one." She started walking and turned

back. "Coming?"

"I'll catch up with you." I tried not to look, but I couldn't help myself. I looked up and my eyes landed on her hips. For the first time, I understood what my dad meant about my mother. I pulled on my collar and headed to the bar.

chapter six

gabriella

I LOOKED AROUND THE BALLROOM for Phillippe, but didn't see him. I sat down with both my bears and waited for Tony to come back from the buffet. When he returned, I set out to find Phillippe. I did a turn around the room but didn't see him. I went outside and found him in the courtyard. I thought he was on the phone, so I proceeded carefully. I tapped him on the shoulder and he turned around.

"Are you okay?"

"Yes, I just needed some air." I stood next to him. "Did Tony get your bear?"

"Yes." I smiled. "Now I have a pair. I'm going to donate them to the nursery department at my church." I looked up at the sky. "What a beautiful night. The stars are so bright. Did you eat?"

"I wasn't hungry." He sipped from the short clear glass.

I looked at my watch. "What time do you want to leave?"

"Whenever you want to."

He seemed different and he wasn't looking at me. "Are you sure you're all right?"

"We need to keep things professional."

"What are you talking about?"

"This is a business event, and I don't think it's appropriate for you to react like you did earlier back at the game."

What the crap is he talking about? He's the one that's had his eyes plastered to my behind all night. He's the one that picked me up and hugged me. He's the one that almost kissed me in a room full of his colleagues. He bought the dress and told me to make sure I kicked it up a notch so I could make a good impression. Keep your cool girl. Talk about a fast way to kill a crush.

"I understand. Excuse me." I went inside, by passed the ballroom and headed to the taxi stand. I saw Tony as I was getting into a taxi and ignored him.

When I got back to the hotel, I took the beautiful fuchsia dress off and left it in a puddle in the middle of the floor. I got in bed and tried to fall asleep, but Phillippe kept appearing in my head. That almost kiss and how it felt to be wrapped in his arms was on a loop in my mind. The more it played, the more excited I got. Around two o'clock, I realized this wasn't a crush, but something more.

When I woke up, I looked at the dress on the floor and all the messages I had from Phillippe and got angry all over again. How dare he make it seem like I was the one brushing up on him. If I didn't like this job, I'd quit. *God, give me the strength to deal with my boss and not let anger take over. I don't know what his problem is, so I'll let you handle him while I do my job.*

The phone started ringing. I reached over and picked it up. "Hello."

"Good morning, Miss Townsend, feeling better?" Tony asked.

"What…oh…uhm, yes, thank you."

"I told Mr. Marchant you left early because you weren't feeling well. I knocked on your door last night, but there was no answer. I figured you probably took something to help you sleep, right?"

"Yes."

"Can I get you anything?"

"No. Are we still meeting at eight thirty?"

"No. Mr. Marchant had to meet with James Marshall this morning. He said for you to get some rest and he'll meet you in the lobby at ten thirty. Are you sure you're all right?"

"I'm fine. Thank you."

phillippe

"What happened?" Tony growled.

"What do you mean?"

"I saw Gabriella get in a taxi and leave. What happened?"

"I told her we needed to be professional and that it wasn't appropriate for her to be all up on me. Where's the waiter?" I looked around.

"What's wrong with you?"

"There's nothing wrong with me."

He nodded. "Is that why you barely said two words in the car?

"What are you talking about?"

"I saw how you looked at her."

"I don't know what you're talking about." When Gabriella's soft body pressed against mine, it caused a reaction I hadn't expected.

"Come on man. I know what you're doing."

"What am I doing?"

"I'm your boy. I saw what Chantal did to you, but you can't think every woman is like her."

"You're talking out of your…"

"I see how you are with Gabriella."

"What are you talking about?"

"Why didn't you kiss her?"

I shook my head. "I don't know what it is, but I can't get her out of my head. Even when I'm asleep, she's right there. Man, those curves and lips are torturing me. Then she goes and does that thing with her hair." I rubbed my forehead. "I was cool until I got a glimpse of her thighs. Man…I keep telling myself, look, but don't touch. I know the minute I cross that line, one of us could get hurt."

"Or, it could be the ride of your life."

"She's not even my type."

"Maybe that's your problem…she's different and it scares you."

"What…get out of here. I'm not scared of that petite, innocent looking…uhm…" I tugged on my collar.

Tony shook his head smiling. "Think about it. You're used to the model-looking bubble head."

"That's not true."

"Let me see, there was Katrina, whose life ambition was to be a reality tv star. Or Gretchen. I think she said her favorite meal was skrimp scampanini." I started laughing. "Wait a minute, and let's not forget Amber, who signed her name with a letter 'A' inside of a heart. She said it was her *logo*." We laughed harder.

"I get your point."

"True, they were all fine, until you got to know them. Then they just looked ordinary. I think you stuck with Chantal because she was the first one who had a brain. Too bad she didn't have a heart."

I nodded. He was right. None of them could hold a candle to Gabriella. "Man, but she's so young."

"Not really."

"You think I'm being an ass?"

"I know you are."

chapter seven

gabriella

I SAT IN THE LOBBY waiting on Phillippe. I was still a little heated from last night. I closed my eyes and prayed softly. *God, forgive me for acting like a child. Please don't let me say anything that could jeopardize my job. Amen.*

I needed a distraction from the drama and opened my iPad. I tried reading, but my thoughts were focused elsewhere. How is it possible for me to have developed such strong feelings for Phillippe after just a few weeks? Yes, he's fine, sensitive, smart, funny, charismatic and...why am I torturing myself? There is no reason or explanation other than it just happened.

I should have answered at least one of his calls last night, or listened to one of his messages. I don't like not being prepared for a meeting. Being pissed off is one thing. Being unprofessional is not acceptable.

I wasn't sure where we were going today, so I didn't know how to prepare. I may have, if I hadn't been so stubborn.

Suddenly, a shadow blocked the sunlight that was shining down on me. I looked up and Phillippe was standing next to me. Crap. How are we supposed to keep things professional, if he insists on looking so freaking hot all the time?

"Mind if I join you?" I pointed to the empty chair across from me and closed my iPad. He sat down and took off his sunglasses. His cologne surrounded the intimate space. I took a deep breath and tried not to let his gorgeous face distract me. "I want to apologize for my behavior last night. It wasn't you, it was me. My last relationship left me with a lot of scars and I'm a little…"

"Scared."

"Cautious." He nodded with a slight smile. "You came in here and shook up my world. I've been trying to fight these feelings I have for you, but they won't go away." He moved to the edge of the chair. "I need you on my team, but more importantly, I want you in my life. So how do we handle this?"

I bit my bottom lip and looked into his eyes. "You're assuming I feel the same."

"Don't tell me I just poured my heart out and you…" He dropped his head and clasped his hands.

I reached over and covered his hands with mine. He slowly raised his head and looked me in the eye. "I like my job and I like you. Maybe we take it slow and figure the rest out as we go?"

He lifted my hand to his lips and gently kissed it. Then he brushed his lips against my ear and I gasped. His spicy manly scent and the heat of his sweet breath was overwhelming. His cheek grazed mine as he whispered, "I can do that."

phillippe

God, I can't believe I fell in love with this woman. It hasn't even been a month and I can't imagine my life without her. I need you to help me fix the mess I made with Gabriella.

I had a hard time concentrating at my meeting. All I could think about was Gabriella and how desperate I am to fix things with her.

After meeting with James, I went up to Pediatrics. Walking around, observing the children and their families, reminded me of my conversation with Gabriella. Listening to her talk about the children she works with at her church inspired me.

I called James and told him I wanted to add an art room and a museum to showcase the children's art. We could ask local artists to come in and help with art therapy. He thought it was a great idea. I can't wait to tell Gabriella...that is, if she's speaking to me.

I walked into the lobby and saw her sitting off to the side by herself and knew I was ready for this relationship. I was up most of the night thinking about her. She crossed her legs and before she pulled her skirt down, I caught a glimpse of her thigh. How is it possible that this woman has had me all twisted up?

She was pretty angry last night, and she had every right to be. I acted like a jerk. I can't believe my best friend called me an ass, but he's right. I have to stop comparing every woman to Chantal. I also have to face up to my part in the demise of our relationship. I could have been a little more open. But she didn't have to say my decision to take this offer was a step down.

It's not a step down, but a welcome challenge. She failed to understand how important loyalty is to me. If she had, then we'd still be together and I'd have another person I could trust on my team. Instead, she opted to stay at Thomas Childs and break up with me. Good thing I never proposed or agreed to her idea of living together. That greedy chick would have kept the ring and probably sued me for the apartment. As it is, I regret having bought her a place in my building. An upside to this long trip is I don't have to bump into her every day. I'd move, but I like my place and the view is amazing.

Here I am walking over to a woman I've known for less than a month, prepared to beg her forgiveness and a chance at sharing my life with her. I don't know who this man is, but I think I might like him.

I stopped next to her chair, cleared my throat and she looked up at me with those big, beautiful brown eyes. At that moment, I was prepared do whatever she asked of me.

chapter eight

gabriella

PHILLIPPE SAID WE WOULD BE staying over an extra day. He gave me no instructions so I wasn't able to prepare. My phone rang at seven, and I recognized the ringtone and pressed the answer call button.

"Hello."

"Good morning, Miss Townsend."

"Good morning, Tony."

"Mr. Marchant wants you to meet him in the lobby in an hour for a breakfast meeting."

"Okay."

"And dress casual."

"Casual?" Strange order.

"Yes. He said you will be doing a lot of walking after the meeting."

"All right." I got up and got dressed.

I stood in the lobby looking for Tony and Phillippe, but didn't see either of them. I walked out to the valet stand and saw the car, but neither of them. I headed back inside and heard a horn honk and someone call my name. I turned around and it was Phillippe in a vintage white Cadillac convertible.

"What's this?" I smiled. "Tony said we have a breakfast meeting?"

"We do." He got out of the car and walked over and hugged me. "Good morning."

"Good morning. What's going on?"

"You and I are going to breakfast. I heard about this place about twenty minutes away that serves the best biscuits and gravy." He escorted me to the car.

"What do you know about biscuits and gravy?" I teased.

"Girl, you'd be surprised at the things you don't think I should know, but do." He winked and opened the door. I got into the car, he closed the door, walked around to the driver's side and got in behind the wheel. "Ready?"

"Miss Townsend."

I turned and saw Tony walking towards the car. "I'll take your bag." He reached into the back seat and picked up my tote bag. "Have fun." He smiled.

"Bye."

It was a beautiful day. I looked at Phillippe and couldn't believe how my life had changed in such a short time.

We pulled into a parking lot next to a little grey building. He got out, walked around and helped me out of the car. "My hair must look a mess." I reached into my bag for something to pull my hair back and found a barrette. I tried to smooth my hair back.

He reached up and stopped me. "You look beautiful."

"I feel like it's a wild mess."

He eased his fingers along the nape of my neck and up the back of my head. The heat of his fingers penetrated my scalp, sending a charge straight to my core. He gently combed through my hair with his fingers, arranging the curls on my shoulder. He stepped closer and I found myself mesmerized by his smile and gentleness as he repeated the move. He leaned in close and my heart started racing anticipating the feel of his lips against mine. He lifted my chin up and slowly lowered his mouth. A horn sounded and he pulled away.

∞ ⤸ ∞ ⤸ ∞ ⤸ ∞

After stuffing ourselves with biscuits, gravy and scrambled eggs, we drove a little while. Phillippe covered my hand with his and it just felt right…comfortable.

"I have a surprise for you," Phillippe smiled.

What could top this spontaneous date? Shortly after he made that announcement, we pulled off the main road and drove a little. We stopped at a big red and white barn, got out, walked inside, and I couldn't believe what I saw.

"How did you find a museum in the middle of nowhere?"

"Let's just say, the concierge earned her tip." He smiled and winked." We stopped at the information desk. "Phillippe Marchant, I booked a private tour."

"Your guide will be right with you."

"Thank you."

We walked around the bright gallery admiring the

paintings while waiting for our tour guide.

"Mr. Marchant," the woman at the information desk called out.

Phillippe walked over to the desk and I continued walking around. An interesting landscape caught my attention. I snapped a few pictures and continued walking around.

I looked up and saw Phillippe walking towards me, and my body started to tremble. The closer he got the hotter my face felt. He stopped in front of me, slipped his hand around my waist and pulled me to his chest. With his other hand, he gently brushed my hair back, never breaking eye contact. He lowered his face to mine, and the exotic spices of his cologne framed the mood as he gently grazed my lips with his. Everything inside of me was on fire.

"You're beautiful."

He grabbed my lips between his, teasing and demanding more. The way the heat of his body mixed with his cologne was intoxicating and overwhelming. He gently glided his tongue along my bottom lip, teasing me even more. He pulled me closer and I could feel every muscle in his chest and thighs pressed against me. Breathing was becoming a challenge.

Those lips I had been fantasizing about were grazing mine just enough, so that I could feel their softness. I opened my mouth slightly, giving him permission to take our kiss further and deeper.

He covered my mouth with his and it was better than I had imagined. He tasted like ginger and honey. His warm tongue started a gentle dance with mine as it searched for that sweet spot. One hand moved down the small of my back pulling me deeper into his space, as his other hand buried itself in the thick curls on the back of my head.

The heat of his fingers and the warm fullness of his

tongue moving in sync sparked some strange feelings. My body tingled from top to bottom, and I didn't want him to stop. At that moment, I didn't care about the art on the walls. The only art I wanted to experience was more of his kiss.

I reached my hands around his neck and pulled him closer so I could enjoy the taste of him.

Suddenly, a female voice called out, "Excuse me… excuse me…"

We broke the kiss, looked around, and a middle aged woman was looking at us. I covered my mouth with my hand, a little embarrassed at our behavior.

"Excuse me sir," she repeated.

Phillippe cleared his throat and addressed the woman. "Yes."

"I'll be your guide…that is if you're still interested in the tour."

He looked at me, then back at her. "Yes, we are, thank you," he smiled.

"Fine, you might want to wipe that lipstick off your face." She commented with a disapproving look.

"Yes ma'am." I looked at him, smiling. He took my hand and we followed our tour guide.

There was some amazing art in that old barn, but all I could think about was that kiss. After the tour, we did a little sightseeing. It was late when we finally made it back to the hotel. Phillippe walked me to my room and we stopped in front of my door.

"So what happens now?" I asked.

He stepped closer and I backed up against the wall. "What do you mean?" He brushed my hair behind my shoulder.

"I had an amazing time today, but we never discussed how we're going to…"

He kissed my neck. "Work together and…"

"Exactly."

"I thought we agreed to take it slow."

I patted his chest. My God, this man is solid. "We did, but…"

He slid his hand around my waist and pulled me to his chest. I wrapped my arms around his neck, looked into his eyes searching for an answer to my question. He captured my lips between his, kissing me deep and hard. His hands traveled down my back and grabbed my behind. I gasped at the foreign touch and pulled back. I looked into his eyes and they seemed darker, more seductive, intense. I bit my lip wondering if I should continue or call it a night.

He lowered his forehead to mine and his hot espresso scented breath and intoxicating cologne produced a heady euphoria I liked. "Do you want me to come inside?"

I closed my eyes, knowing if I looked at him, I might say yes. "No," I replied and opened my eyes.

He moved those sexy swollen lips to my neck and I let out another gasp. I tried to get some air, but I couldn't. "Are you sure?"

I swallowed hard. The good girl was wrestling with the bad girl. The good girl, said, "No." The bad girl, said, "It's better to kiss in private." He glided his hot finger along my arm and I wanted to jump out of my skin.

"Uhm…I…I…" He nibbled my ear. Oh man. "I think…"

"Gabriella, nous a laissés embrasser dans privé, mon amour…" followed by a kiss on my neck.

French, you have got to be kidding. I cupped his face in my hands and gently pressed my lips against his. "Good night."

"Good night?"

I bit my lip and nodded. "Good night."

He leaned back and smiled. "Where's your key?"

"Why?"

"Gabriella, give me your key." He stepped back and the smile was gone. I handed him my key, he opened the door and gently pushed me inside.

"What happened?"

"I asked could I come inside and you said no."

"So you're leaving?"

"We agreed to take it slow. You're right, my coming inside definitely isn't taking it slow. It's something that could be a little dangerous."

"What's that supposed to mean? You know what, never mind. Good night." I slammed the door.

How dare he think I would sleep with him! I threw my bag on the chair and paced back and forth. That man! And where did the French come from? Not only do I have to figure him out in English, now I have to know French too.

Knock…knock…knock… "Gabriella, open the door."

"No," I shouted back. A few seconds later the door opened. I turned around and he was standing in front of the closed door. "How did you get in here?"

"You forgot to take the key." I walked over, snatched the key and he pulled me to his chest and kissed me so hard I forgot why I was angry. He slowly pulled back and stroked the side of my face. "Mon Amour, may I explain?"

Still heady from the kiss, I could barely get my reply out. "Su…su…sure."

He smiled. "I thought some privacy would be better, but you were right." I felt like an idiot. He brushed my lips with the ball of his thumb. "You're not the kind of girl who wants to be on display. I apologize, but I couldn't help myself. Those lips were calling me."

I smiled. "I'm sorry. I thought you were trying to get me in bed."

"The thought occurred to me."

"Oh."

He gently brushed my cheek. "I'm not going to lie. There is nothing that would delight me more, than to share my bed with you." He brushed my lips with the tip of his finger.

"I...I...,"

"Shhh...let's not cloud our minds with something that's not relevant at the moment. Okay, Mon Amour?" He moved his mouth along my jaw, before covering my mouth with his in an amazing kiss.

phillippe

I can't believe she shut me down. The way she kissed me, I just knew...I thought we were on the same page. I heard the words come out of her mouth, but her body said something completely different. The way her body molded to mine as we kissed, I just knew I'd be in her room right now tasting every inch of her.

No...that's what she said. I think she's the first woman to not invite me in. What's even worse, I'm not upset. In fact, her rejecting my suggestion makes me want her even more. True, I'm headed back to my suite to take a long, cold shower, but I'm good.

I walked into the suite and Tony was sitting on the sofa

watching television. He looked at his watch. "What are you doing back so early?"

I closed the door, took my jacket off and rolled up my sleeves. "Uhm…" I grabbed a bottle of mineral water and drank it in one shot.

Tony pressed the pause button on the remote and placed his bowl of popcorn on the table. "Okay, what happened? Did you decide to skip dinner?"

I grabbed another bottle of water and walked over to the chair next to the sofa and sat down. "We had dinner, it's dessert we skipped."

"Let's back up. Did she have a good time?"

"She said she enjoyed herself."

"Good, so why are you here and not with Gabriella?"

I took a long sip from my bottle. "I walked her back to her room…everything was going fine. We were kissing and I suggested we go inside where it was private and she said no."

"No?"

"No." I nodded. "I can't…I mean, I know she was feeling me, but she said *no*." He smiled. "What's so funny?"

"You."

"Me?"

"You really thought she was going to sleep with you?"

"I mean…I thought…I wasn't proposing sex. I was suggesting privacy."

He shook his head. "That's what you want to go with?"

"Yeah. I thought she would have been more comfortable in her room."

"You have an MBA, right?"

"What does that have to do with this conversation?"

"Hear me out. Gabriella isn't a dime a dozen chick. She doesn't need you."

"I don't understand."

She may be attracted to you. Heck, she may even have feelings for you. But her career means more to her than sleeping with some slick, rich dude."

"Excuse me?"

"Today was a step in the right direction, but you've just begun your hike to get her heart."

"You lost me."

"The women in your past relationships were fine with only the material things and a portion of you. Gabriella, doesn't care about the things. She wants to know you. If you want her, you have got to share you with her."

"Crap!" I can't believe my best friend is laughing at me. "What's so funny?"

"She's got your number."

"What do you mean?"

"Think about it. You said she enjoyed the date."

"Yes."

"Let me ask, how was the kiss?" I couldn't look at him. I turned my bottle up and finished it. "That good?"

"I didn't say anything."

"You didn't have to. It's all over your face." He sipped his ginger ale. "She asked how you two were going to handle work and a personal relationship."

"What did you say?"

"Slowly."

"That's not an answer, it's an adverb." He shook his head. "She wanted to hear your plan for the two of you."

"My plan?"

"You approached her, which meant you had a plan."

"Crap!"

"You need to let her dictate the course of the

relationship…set the pace and when she's ready, she'll let you in. Metaphorically speaking."

"Great. So what am I suppose to do while I wait on her to *metaphorically* let me in?"

"Court her."

"What?"

"Go old school. Make it about her…Throw on the charm."

I stood up. "Charm her…I can do that." I started towards my bedroom.

"Turning in?"

"Right after my very cold shower."

∞ ⅊ ∞ ⅊ ∞ ⅊ ∞

Gabriella asked the million dollar question, "How are we going to work together and be in a personal relationship?" I failed to answer her question.

Before she came into my life, I was content with being alone for a little while. After spending three tumultuous years with Chantal, the last thing I wanted was to be in another relationship.

Gabriella has changed that for me. She brings passion and excitement to my life. I've never had a woman effect me the way she does. She consumes my thoughts and my dreams. I find myself lying in bed fantasizing about her. How she'll feel lying underneath me…what she'll sound like when we make love, and how those beautiful thighs will feel wrapped around me. When I do fall asleep, Gabriella is there with those lips and hips doing things no good girl should know anything about.

I'm not sure where this relationship is headed, but for

the first time, I see marriage as an option and I don't feel like I'm being pushed. However, before I can entertain that, I need to get this company healthy. When I agreed to take over, I was assured the board would be very supportive. Now that things are underway, the person that I thought would have my back, is giving me the most headaches.

My grandfather has got to step back and let me do the job he hired me to do. Otherwise, I'm stepping down and he can get someone else to be the CEO of Morgan Grant.

chapter nine
gabriella

I SLAPPED MY ALARM AND reluctantly sat up, stretched my hands over my head, and let out a long yawn. *"Thank you, God for another beautiful day."* I climbed out of bed and went into the bathroom. I bypassed the mirror, went straight to the toilet, and then the shower. After the hot water danced along my body, reality set in. I was now dating my boss…I think.

I turned the shower off, climbed out, grabbed a towel and wrapped it around my body. I walked over to the vanity, wiped the dew-covered glass, looked at my reflection and repeated the words. "I'm dating my boss…what the crap!"

Last night, back it up, yesterday, it seemed like a good idea, especially after he kissed me. Then last night when he walked me to my room and kissed me again, it really seemed like a good idea. Now, after a restless night, I'm wondering if dating my boss is a good idea. *"God what have I done?"*

I got dressed and continued praying. My phone rang and I almost jumped out of my skin. I stopped packing and stared at the phone. It rang again so I walked over and picked it up. "Hello Miss Townsend, this is your wake up call." I forgot I requested a wake up call.

"Thank you." I put the receiver down and sat on the edge of the bed with my head in my hands. This is a bad idea. What if it doesn't work? I don't know anything about Phillippe other than he likes the color black, art, and when he kisses me, my entire body ignites. If this thing tanks, I could lose my job. I've worked too hard to lose everything behind a powerful set of lips and a tight behind. I've got to fix this before...

My phone rang with Phillippe's ring tone. I hesitated to answer. After the third ring I pressed the Accept Call button. "Hello."

"Good morning, Mon Amour."

"Good morning."

"We'll be leaving in thirty minutes. Do you need more time?"

That was new. Usually, he tells me what time to meet him. After one date, things are already changing. "No, that will be fine."

"We'll have breakfast on the plane."

"Okay."

"I've already called the bellman for you."

"Thank you. Bye."

"Bye." Click.

∞ ?⅊∞ ?⅊∞ ?⅊∞

The bellman loaded the last of my bags on the cart and left. I walked around and double checked all the drawers and closets. I picked up my tote bag and purse and opened the door.

"What are you doing here Phillippe? I thought we were meeting downstairs?"

"May I come in?"

There's that question from last night. "Sure." I stepped to the side, closed the door and put my bags on the chair.

"After I hung up, I sensed there was something bothering you."

"There's nothing…" I folded my arms in front of my chest, a definite contradiction to my statement.

"Please, let me finish." He stepped closer and my heart leapt to my throat. "I was up most of the night thinking about your question."

"My question?"

"Yes. You asked how we were going to handle our relationship."

"You said, we would take it slowly."

"That's not an answer, it's an adverb." I smiled. "I was caught up in the moment and…I know the policy is that any Executive involved with an employee on any level has to inform Human Resources. However, if you don't mind, I would prefer to wait a while before putting our relationship under the Human Resources microscope."

"I agree."

"As for the office. What do you suggest? What would make you comfortable?"

He caught me off guard with that question. One of my concerns about our work relationship was not being the center of office gossip. It hadn't occurred to me that our plan needed to include how we would handle office protocol. I definitely don't think now is the proper time to ask my mother for help.

"I think we need to keep it professional. That doesn't mean I expect you to call me Miss Townsend, or me call you Mr. Marchant."

"I don't know, calling you Miss Townsend has a little naughty vibe to it." He smiled. "First names it is."

"What if this tanks?"

"If you're asking will you lose your job? The answer is no. If this falls apart, I'll promote you to another department."

"So it's a win win situation for me." I smiled and dropped my arms. I was starting to feel better about this whole thing.

"You could say that." He stepped closer.

"It's imperative we keep our two worlds separate. If we are fighting, we have to leave it outside of the building."

"I agree." He stroked the side of my face. "I promise not to attack those gorgeous lips during work hours."

"Will Tony always travel with us?"

"Do you have a problem with Tony?"

"No. I like Tony, and think it would…"

"You feel more comfortable having him around?"

"Yes."

"Then it's done. Anything else?" He stepped closer and took my hands in his.

"I need you to understand I'm not like the other women you've dated." I tried not to fidget. "Yesterday, you said you wanted to share your bed with me."

"I shouldn't have said that." He stepped closer. "I like

you. I want this thing with us to work…but only if you do."

I looked at him searching those gorgeous dark eyes for his truth. I cleared my throat and continued. "I do, but I need you to understand that I can't give you what you probably had in your past relationships…that's not me."

I hope he understands what I'm trying to say. Although I am deeply attracted to him and my mind fills with all kinds of wicked thoughts when I'm around him, and his kisses turn my insides to hot jelly, I can't sleep with him.

"I understand. I respect your honesty." He stroked the side of my face. "I'm prepared for this. It just means, I'll be spending a lot more time in the gym and taking a lot of cold showers." He teased. "Gabriella, I like you and I promise not to push you to do anything you don't want to do. Anything else?"

I stepped closer, and the heat of his body surrounded me. He pulled me to his chest and brushed the side of my face with his lips. I wanted to sink deep into his space. He grabbed my lips between his and kissed me like he did last night.

There was a knock on the door followed by a familiar voice. "Miss Townsend." Another knock.

"Yes, Tony…"

"Have you seen Mr. Marchant?" he called out. We pulled apart and I walked over and opened the door.

"Good morning, Tony."

"Good morning, Miss Townsend. Have you seen Mr. Marchant?" I opened the door wider and Phillippe walked around and stood in the middle of the room. Tony looked at Phillippe and then back at me. "I'll meet both of you downstairs in ten minutes."

"I'm…we were…"

"We'll be right down, Tony," Phillippe answered. Tony

looked at Phillippe with a raised eyebrow and left.

I closed the door and grabbed my chest breathing hard. "What did you tell him?" The last thing I need is for Tony to look at me with a disapproving eye because I'm dating my boss.

Phillippe walked over, wrapped me in his arms, brushed his tongue across my lips and kissed me. "I told him we're taking it slow."

phillippe

I rolled over and tried to sleep, but every time I closed my eyes, Gabriella was there with those sexy lips and those dangerous hips. She's got me all tied up in knots and now the not sleeping is getting worse. I was getting a few torturous hours. Now, I'm sleeping like a baby…two hours here and then up for one. This ongoing agony is killing me.

I bet she's sound asleep, secure in knowing she's got the upper hand. I could try another cold shower, but what good would that do? I'd just be cold and wide awake with the only warm solution guaranteed to help me sleep at the end of the hall.

"No." The sound of her sweet and innocent voice uttering that powerful two letter word is like an anvil landing on my foot. I know she said it, because I saw her lips move as the word floated off her lips. In the past, when I asked, well I didn't really ask, it was more like me taking the liberty of inviting myself in, I was always received with open arms. And not for a hit and run, but for the night.

And when there was a little apprehension, I simply dropped a few words of French. I myself am amazed at how powerful the French language is. The French side of me is well versed in the art of seduction. A few choice words in French, a little ear nibbling and a gentle stroke of the arm at the door and I'm in for the night. None of that worked with Gabriella.

∞ ⅔ ∞ ⅔ ∞ ⅔ ∞

I rolled over and slapped my clock. It was six thirty. I'm not sure what time Gabriella finally left my dreams and allowed me some sleep.

After a quick workout, I got dressed and called Gabriella. Her distant tone left an uneasy feeling with me.

"What's wrong?" Tony asked.

"I'm not sure." I looked at my watch. "I'll be right back." I picked up my jacket and left.

I hurried down to her room, and stopped at the door. I took a deep breath and knocked hard, but there was no answer. I started to walk away, but I wanted to settle this before we left, and in private. I knocked again.

When she opened the door, she took my breath away. Even in casual clothes, her curves were evident. Once I surveyed her body from the ground up and met her eyes, what I sensed was on her face. She looked distressed and I'm pretty sure I was the cause for the furrowed brow.

I wanted to scoop her up in my arms and tell her everything was going to be fine and to trust me. I realized there were only nine words that would alleviate her obvious anxiety, *"You will not be fired if this doesn't work."* When I made my promise, her body and face quickly relaxed and I was treated to a smile.

I went a step further and took Tony's advice and asked her how she wanted to conduct our personal relationship. I think I caught her off guard. Who knew being open would yield the results I got. When she stepped to me, I got a surprise I wasn't expecting.

Her honesty about our not sleeping together did two things to me. One, it made me respect her even more. And second, it made me want her even more. Those simple words, conjured up visions of her lying underneath me bringing her so much pleasure she would be begging me not to stop.

I closed my eyes and when I looked up she had invaded my space. I pulled her to me, crushed my lips against hers, taking her mouth and tongue, leading them in a passionate dance. Her response was immediate. She pulled me closer and treated me to a slight moan of approval inside my mouth. If this kiss had happened a couple of months ago, we'd be prostrate on the floor with her gorgeous thick thighs wrapped around my hips and us crying out in pleasure together.

I couldn't seem to get enough of her. A knock broke through the euphoria, and I tried to ignore it. Another knock followed by, "Miss Townsend."

chapter ten

gabriella

WE FINALLY MADE IT BACK home and I was exhausted. I've stayed in some amazing hotels, but I missed my bed. It was difficult getting used to no room service or turn down service. However, I wouldn't be home long enough for my old daily routine to reattach itself to me.

When we landed, Phillippe told me to take a couple of days off and rest. I was a little surprised he didn't drive me home. Instead, Tony dropped me off reiterating Phillippe's instructions.

I tried not to let it bother me that he didn't drive me home. I took a bath and crashed deciding to deal with Phillippe and my luggage tomorrow.

I was awakened from my sound sleep by someone

shaking me. "Gabby…Gabby…wake up, baby. Your phone is ringing."

I rolled over and wiped my eyes. "What?"

"You left your phone on the counter. I think it's your boss." She handed me the phone and walked out, closing the door behind her.

I opened my eyes wide as if that would help me see the screen easier through the layer of sleep distorting my vision. I checked the voicemail and there were three voicemails and six texts from Phillippe. I pressed his number and the loud ringing sent a sharp pang to my ear.

"Mon Amour, are you alright? I've been trying to reach you for a few hours."

Am I alright? You'd know if you brought me home and not had one of your henchmen deliver me like a call girl after she fulfilled her assignment. "I was sleeping." I think we need to rethink this whole personal relationship thing. Last time I checked, I thought it was customary for a boyfriend to take his girlfriend home from the airport, not have her… "What do you want Phillippe?"

"I wanted to make sure we were still on for dinner tonight?"

"We don't have anything scheduled for tonight."

"Did you get the flowers?"

"What flowers…what are you talking about?" I sat up.

"That's why I had Tony take you home."

"You lost me."

"Did you get the flowers?" he repeated.

"Hold on." I looked around my room and didn't see any flowers. I climbed out of bed, put my robe on and went downstairs. "Mom."

"I'm in here, baby," she called out.

I went into the kitchen and stopped at the counter. My eyes almost popped out of their sockets. It was a huge arrangement of white lilies and roses.

"When did these come?"

"Before I went to my meeting." She took her jacket off and placed it on the chair. "I figured you'd see them when you came downstairs. You must be exhausted."

"I uhm…" I reached up for the small black envelope, opened it and pulled out the simple white card. *Welcome to the team. Good first month. Phillippe.* "Oh crap! I left him on hold." I ran back up to my room.

I picked up my phone. "The flowers are beautiful, but I don't see anything about tonight."

"I thought you would have called as soon as you read the card."

"I'm sorry. The flowers came while I was asleep."

"No, it's my fault. I was trying to surprise you." Now I felt bad. I was unduly angry and possibly missed out on a great dinner. "I know you want to keep things private that's why I didn't…when you called me, I was going to tell you about dinner."

"Tony didn't mention anything."

"That's because I didn't tell him."

"Is it too late?" It was six and it wouldn't take me long to get dressed.

"Are you sure you feel up to it? We can do it another time."

"I'm fine. I've been sleeping since Tony dropped me off."

"Okay, I'll pick you…"

"I'll come to you."

"No, I'll pick you up."

"Please don't. It's too soon. I just don't feel like…"

82

"I'll give in this one time and send Marcos. He'll be there in an hour. See you soon. Bye."

"Bye." I pressed the button ending the call. I looked at the clock and then at my reflection. I looked a hot mess and had an hour to turn myself into something amazing. "Mom," I called out and ran back downstairs. "Mom." I hurried into the kitchen. "Mom."

"Gabriella, stop all that yelling." She continued putting the groceries away. "What's going on?"

"I have to meet my boss for dinner."

"Excuse me?"

"I need your help. A car will be here in an hour to pick me up." I hurried back upstairs and stood in front of my closet looking for something to wear. I threw my suit case on the bed and went searching for the black DVF dress. Crap, it's wrinkled and I need time to get my hair together.

My mother walked into my room. "What is going on?"

"My boss wants me to attend a last minute dinner tonight and I wanted to wear this, but…" I held up the black dress. She walked over and grabbed me by the shoulders.

"Calm down." I took a deep breath. "What did he say?"

"He said he's sending a car to pick me up in an hour."

"Where are you going?"

"I forgot to ask."

"Let me see the dress." I handed her the wrinkled black dress. "I'll work on getting the wrinkles out and you work on getting yourself together."

I kissed her on the cheek. "Thank you, Mommy."

"You're welcome."

∞ ⅔⅝∞ ⅔⅝∞ ⅔⅝∞

I walked into the restaurant and my heart was racing. I felt a little guilty not telling my mom the details of my dinner. I know her and if I told her the truth about this dinner, she'd be sitting in the bar or parking lot watching me.

I stopped at the maitre'd station. "Phillippe Marchant's table."

The grey haired gentleman looked at me and smiled. "This way, Miss." I followed behind him as we walked along the narrow aisle that lead to a private room at the back of the restaurant. He pushed the door open and I walked inside. I looked around and didn't see Phillippe. "Have a seat."

"Thank you. Where is Mr. Marchant?" He answered my question with a smile and left.

I looked around the beautiful dark wood paneled intimate dining room. The small table was dressed in white linens, white china, white roses and soft soulful music was playing. I heard a door open, looked up and Phillippe walked in wearing a white apron tied around his waist. "What's going on?"

"I'll be your server for the first course." He smiled.

It felt like my smile covered my face. "What?"

"I wanted to do something special for our first date." He set the plate of appetizers down, walked around the table, and kissed me. "I have been wanting to do that since this morning."

"Me, too." He took his apron off and sat down. "You know this isn't our first date."

"It's the first one that counts." He smiled as he poured each of us a glass of wine.

"So what are we having?"

THE GOOD GIRL

"For our first course, we have a plate of assorted appetizers…Grilled Crostini with Burrata, Figs, & Prosciutto, Herb Blinis with Smoked Salmon and Creme Fraiche, Roasted Lamb Ribs with Jalapeno Mint Sauce and Roasted Beet & Herbed Goat Cheese Napoleon."

The past month I have stepped way outside of my food comfort zone and tried some foods I don't think I would have ever tried, if Phillippe hadn't persuaded me. "I'll try the blinis." I reached for it and he stopped me.

"I'll serve." He picked up a blini. "Open your mouth." I hesitated at first and then I complied. He placed the petite bit on my tongue. I closed my eyes absorbing the flavors as I chewed. "What do you think?"

"Incredible."

A couple of hours later, we had finished three more courses and were enjoying some cheese and wine. "Tonight is the first time I've seen you drink wine."

"We were working and I didn't think it was appropriate during business hours."

"But tonight…"

"I'm on a date."He lifted my hand to his mouth and kissed it.

"Tomorrow, I thought we…" His phone started vibrating on the table. He looked at the screen and pressed the ignore call button. "I thought it would be nice if we…" His phone buzzed with a text and he looked at the screen. "I'm sorry. I really need to deal with this."

"I understand. Where's the ladies' room?"

He walked around the table, kissed me on the neck and pulled out my chair. Then he opened the door and pointed. "It's at the end of the hall."

"Thank you."

phillippe

Planning this date has been more stressful than any other date I've planned. If Gabriella were like my past companions, I'd fly her to Vegas for dinner and a show. And if she were so inclined, we'd stay the night, possibly longer.

I should be upset that Gabriella doesn't expect a lot from me, but it's like Tony said, she's not impressed by the *things*. I have dated girls who had the audacity to email pictures of the latest bags, shoes and things they wanted me to buy for them. These women would jump at the chance to join the private jet mile high club, or willingly offer me limo sex. Gabriella isn't like that. I had to force her to take that gown and wear it to a work function.

I didn't push the issue of not picking her up, because right now I'm letting her call the shots until she feels comfortable and trusts me.

I set this date up a couple of days ago, and for a minute there, it looked like it was all for nothing. I think the reason I'm so nervous is because being intimate on a level that does not include my body, is foreign to me.

I opened this restaurant because I love good food and wine. The other times I've brought dates here, I never went out on limb like I am tonight. This is a woman I see a future with. I remember something my dad said. *"When you find the woman you are willing to completely change for, that's the one. And do whatever it takes to keep her."* So if that means learning to be celibate, then so be it. The prize is well worth the wait.

"She's here, Phillippe," Tomas announced.

With those three words all talking in the kitchen ceased. It's as if we'd just been informed royalty had entered the restaurant. In a way it had. The woman I desire to make the queen of my world has just been seated. "Thank you Tomas." I looked at Chef Paul. "Give us about twenty minutes and then bring out the next course and the wine. Thank you, chef." I grabbed the plate of appetizers and wine.

"Bon appetite." The conversation and bustle of the kitchen resumed.

A couple of hours later with three additional courses completed, we sat back and enjoyed some cheese and wine.

"Everything was amazing."

"I'm glad you liked it."

She looked around the room and sipped her wine. "Nice place for a first date."

I lifted her hand to my mouth, kissed it and started to share details about our adventure tomorrow when my phone started vibrating. I ignored it, because I sensed it was bad news and I didn't want anything to overshadow my time with Gabriella. However, when my phone buzzed with Tony's ringtone, I knew I couldn't ignore whatever it was. I told him not to text or call me tonight unless it was an emergency. I looked at the screen.

"I'm sorry, I really need to deal with this."

Gabriella excused herself and went to the ladies' room. That gave me time to call Tony back. I pressed the button and had an uneasy feeling as I dialed the number.

"Hello…I'm at dinner…did you tell them we have a signed lease and if they go back on our agreement, I'll tie them up in so much…I don't care…no…this is why I need someone in place I can trust…he did what…why didn't he…that was my final offer…let him…uh-huh…uh-huh…no…when…I don't want to, but…" I looked at my watch. "Crap! Do you have anyone we can put there to oversee the move?…I don't want to do that…I know…I was finishing dinner…I'll call when I'm on my way…I know."

I wanted to throw my phone against the wall. I heard the door open and when I turned around, she took my breath away. I walked over, closed the door, and placed her bag on the edge of the table. I took her in my arms, and we slowly swayed to the soulful music I requested for the evening. She looked up at me smiling. At that moment all I wanted was those lips pressed against mine, before taking complete control of her tongue.

I remember the first time she gave me that look. I covered those full sexy lips with mine not waiting for permission, but going by her body language. She may not want to sleep with me, but I knew she wanted me to kiss her. My hands eased down the small of her back and pulled her so close we seemed to melt into one person. I kissed her harder and she dug her hands into my neck, drawing me deeper into her space.

The chemistry and passion between us is overwhelming. I felt my body starting to react and I didn't want her to think I couldn't control myself, but I wasn't ready to let her go either. I moved my mouth across her cheek, grabbed her ear lobe between my teeth and she let out a deep gasp. Her seductive parfum traveled up my nose and it reignited the fire I was trying to sit on.

My phone rang again with Tony's ringtone and I wanted to curse him for calling me. I knew answering it, meant I would have to be separated from Gabriella's sexy swollen lips. So I ignored it, but it kept ringing.

She pulled back and looked up at me. "You know he won't stop calling until you answer."

I picked up my phone and pressed the button. "Yes... what...no..." I looked at my watch. "I can be there in a couple of hours...I know...bye." I pressed the button ending the call.

"What's wrong?"

"It's Seattle." She patted my chest. "The person I wanted to hire turned down my offer."

"So, go with an interim person until you find a permanent solution."

I love her innocence. I would put her there in the interim, but she's not ready yet. "My first interim choice isn't available."

"The past month I've watched you work, and something as minor as availability isn't going to stop you."

"I've got Tony working on it."

"Problem solved."

"Not exactly. Even if I get an interim person in place by the end of the week, it will take Tony at least two weeks to get them up to speed."

"Then do it."

"You're okay with that?"

"Why wouldn't I be?"

"You said now that our relationship had changed, you would feel better if he traveled with us." I quickly reminded her of her request.

"I would, but..."

I felt her tensing up. "I know I'm asking a lot, but I need you to trust me."

"It's not you I don't trust." She looked up at me with a slight smile.

I leaned back. "You don't trust yourself to be alone with me?"

"Not so much that...it's Paris. I've never been, but I've

heard it's a very romantic city and no matter how good our intentions may be, something could happen."

She caught me off guard with her statement, but she's right. I know she has concerns. The last time I was in Paris, was with Chantal shortly before we broke up. I took her there hoping to rekindle our relationship. Instead, a month after we got back, we broke up. In spite of the tension, we had an amazing time and some of the best sex of our relationship.

"I promise nothing will happen that we don't want to happen."

"Maybe we need to set some rules."

"Rules?" I smiled.

"Yes. No late night walks, picnics, intimate dinners and rooms on separate floors."

"No."

"No?"

"No. I'm not agreeing to any of that."

"I thought we agreed to take our relationship slow?"

"We are. We're both adults and if we can't trust each other, then there's no sense in us going any further with this relationship." I kissed her. "I'm not going to Paris with my girlfriend and treat her like a stranger."

"Girlfriend? That's not a slow word," she smiled.

"For me it is," I smiled.

"I guess my boyfriend is taking me to Paris."

chapter eleven

gabriella

I TRIED TO SNEAK INTO the house. I attribute my stupidity to the wine and the kisses from Phillippe. I walked inside and it was dark except for the light in the kitchen, and the one at the top of the stairs. I turned the lights off and went to my room.

I sat on the side of the bed, replaying the evening and the conversation with Phillippe. He's right. If I'm not going to trust him, I need to walk away now.

I took my phone out of my bag and before I could plug it into the charger, it started vibrating. I pressed the button to read the text...*Mon Amour, I really enjoyed serving and dining with you. Have to cancel our date for tomorrow. On my way to*

Seattle. Will call you later. Bonne nuit, Phillippe. I texted back…
Have a safe trip…Bonne nuit, Gabriella.

I got undressed and climbed into bed. I lay down staring at the ceiling and praying. I know in the morning my mother is going to be full of questions and right now, I don't have suitable answers. I had the truth…I'm dating my boss and while we're in Europe, we're going to really get to know each other. I kept rehearsing my speech until I fell asleep.

I rolled over and the smell of coffee infiltrated my dream and woke me up. I climbed out of bed, went into to the bathroom, brushed my teeth and washed off what was left of last night's makeup. I tamed my wild hair and put on my robe. I looked at my clock. It was nine-thirty. I can't believe I slept that long.

I went downstairs. I was hoping to avoid my mom, but I knew that wasn't possible. When I walked around the corner and into the kitchen, she was standing at the counter reading the paper and drinking coffee. I coughed and she looked up. "Morning, Sunshine or should I say Mon Amour."

My eyes almost popped out of their socket. "Uhm…"

"Coffee?"

"Yes, please." I sat down and she placed a tall white mug in front of me and filled it with hot, black coffee. I took a couple of long sips, hoping the hot liquid would burn my tongue rendering me unable to speak. No such luck. I placed the cup on the counter and looked my mother in the eye.

"Let's talk."

I swallowed hard. My insides were turning, and not in a good way. This wasn't the jumpy, excited stomach I get when I'm with Phillippe. This was the nervous stomach I get when I know I'm about to be interrogated by my mother.

Funny thing, my dad's the lawyer, yet my mother is

much better at extracting information. Maybe she was a spy in her former life. Because no matter how thorough I am in trying to get information out of her, she never cracks. How does she know, Phillippe's pet name for me?

I was scared to take my eyes off of her. I took another couple of sips of caffeine for courage, but I was never any good at playing chicken. "What do you want to talk about?"

"How was dinner?"

This is clearly a trick question. My mother says she never asks a question she doesn't know the answer to. If she's asking me about dinner, then she knows it wasn't a business meeting, but a date.

"Good." I tried not to smile or think about the amazing food and wine or the make out session in the private dining room. I sipped some more coffee.

"Where did you go?"

Another trap. I wish she'd just come right out and ask. But she won't because that would be showing her hand, and she never shows her hand until she's ready.

"I wasn't paying attention when the driver dropped me off."

She nodded. "Really?"

"Yes."

"What time did you get home?"

Okay, I know she knows the answer to this one. I sat up straight and owned my answer. "I got home a little after midnight. How was your evening?...what did you and daddy do?" I tried to shift the focus onto her.

"Your dad turned in early because he had a breakfast meeting, and I sat in bed reading. I must have dosed off right before you got home." She returned her attention to the newspaper. "Any plans today?"

My eyes got wide. How does she know about my date? I swear she has a tracker embedded in me. I sipped some more caffeinated courage and retraced my steps from last night. Then it occurred to me. I vaguely recall her coming in to my room and looking at my phone, but I thought that was a dream.

I pulled my phone out of my pocket and looked at the screen. There was a text from Phillippe…*Good morning, Mon Amour. Should be home late tonight. How about taking our drive and picnic tomorrow? Phillippe.* Crap! Crap! Crap! Busted!

She looked at me and her gaze sent a chill through my body. "So, how much longer do you want to dance around this?"

I placed my phone on the counter and braced myself for this conversation. "What do you want to know?"

the end

find out what happened when

Gabriella and Phillippe went to Europe?

the good girl

book two

EXCERPT FROM

Generational Curse

1

KYLA PROMISED HERSELF SHE WOULD never be like the other women in her family, dating a married man and settling for the pennies he doled out.

She'd always felt she was worth more. She met Eric at a fundraiser. He smiled, she smiled and after the cocktail hour, they found themselves seated next to each other. During dinner they talked and flirted and once the evening was over, he asked for her number. She declined and while getting ready for bed, she reached into her bag for her phone and noticed that she also had someone else's phone.

She called the last number dialed and a vaguely familiar voice said, "I've been waiting for your call. So what time do you want to meet for breakfast so I can get my phone?" They both laughed.

They agreed to meet the following morning for breakfast. Two days later, they met again and included an extra slot for "therapy."

Making love in the morning seemed so decadent. She didn't think anything of it until she received her first black envelope a month later.

Eric said, "I'm tired of hotels. Rent a place and fix it up for us and keep whatever is left."

"I'm not a hooker."

"I didn't mean any disrespect. I want to keep seeing you, but my neighbors are nosey."

"Oh, you're married."

"No, I'm not. I just like my privacy. I like being with you, but—"

"I understand." She dropped her head and quickly began getting dressed. "I don't think this is—"

He noticed the change in her behavior and rushed to reassure her. "I don't want you to think I'm ashamed of you, but I also don't want you to think I'm monopolizing your time. You need your space and so do I. When we get together, it should be on neutral, comfortable ground and not some cold hotel room or a place filled with memories of past lovers."

He wrapped his arms around her pulling her to him, gently stroking her hair, inhaling her neck and gently placing a kiss on her soft shoulder. She turned around trying to read the expression on his face. Looking into his eyes, she wondered how many more love nests he had scattered around the city. She pulled his face close to hers and covering his mouth with hers, kissed him passionately. She slipped her hands inside the front of his pants while sliding her tongue inside his mouth, exciting him to the point of arousal.

She pulled back and whispered, "Once more before we have to go?"

He couldn't resist her. The soft seductive tone of her

voice and the gentle touch of her hand, made him weak and willing to do anything she asked. Kyla knew if there were anyone else, they would have a hard time competing with her.

She got her education in how to manipulate a man by eavesdropping on her aunts' conversations. They were all experts when it came to being with and manipulating married men. She learned how to kiss from her high school boyfriend. And her college boyfriend, her biology professor, schooled her in anatomy and how to physically please a man.

Before getting involved with Eric, she had dated, but she only had two other semi serious relationships. Neither was fulfilling. The first was Thomas Smith. He was cute, but he lacked the drive to satisfy her physically. When they were together she found herself fantasizing about other men. Intellectually he was a genius, but no one really makes love to a person's brain. It was the other part of his body that needed more educating and she knew she wasn't a school teacher.

Then there was Alister Humphrey. The name alone intrigued her. She had never met a black man with such a stuffy name. In the beginning he seemed like the complete package. Model good looks, intelligence and his skills in bed were unbelievable. The first time they made love, the intensity of his being inside her brought tears to her eyes. Not because it was painful, but because she had never felt such pleasure. Alister knew exactly how to read her body. A skill that was the result of his blindness. What he lacked in vision, he more than compensated for in his other senses. But, he was a man and as they all do, he began making demands and that's when she called it quits. Mind blowing sex aside, Kyla was gone.

Her aunts always said, "Don't allow a man to make demands on you. You make the demands on him. Use what you have and any man can be controlled with the sway of your hips and the wink of your eye. And, showing a little cleavage wouldn't hurt either."

If she were going to marry, it would be to Eric. He was everything she wanted. Handsome, well educated, focused, rich and eager to please in and out of bed. But she also learned from her aunts, the wife always got the leftovers and Kyla didn't like leftovers or sloppy seconds. When Eric suggested the apartment, at first she thought, he was ashamed of her. But Eric's response to her kiss and touch convinced her, she was his priority.

She knew she was in charge. She eased her hand further down his pants pleading, "Baby, please make me sing again before sending me off to start the day."

She kissed his neck before dropping the sheet that was caressing her body and walked into the bathroom. He stood still contemplating the repercussions of being late to the office, when he heard the shower running. He looked at his watch and texted his assistant he would be late. He put his phone on the desk, striped, walked into the steam filled bathroom and opened the shower door to a wet and soapy Kyla, smiling.

"Are you ready to sing?" he asked as he leaned her up against the slippery tiled wall. He pressed himself against her and filled his mouth with every inch of her. He lifted her from behind and rode her like a beautiful long legged mare. The harder he rode, the louder she sang. One last trot, and he sang out too. He rested his head on her chest and she had her answer, "no," there was no one else, just her. She reached over and turned the hot water off. They both needed to cool down. "Baby, I'll do whatever you want, just don't leave me," he begged.

She smiled to herself and replied, "Whatever you say baby."

GENERATIONAL CURSE

He pulled away and she turned the hot water back on and washed him like a newborn baby. Gently stroking every inch of him. He knew there wasn't another woman like her. No woman ever treated him like this. He stood still and let her soft hands wash him clean.

On his way to work, he called her. "You are an amazing woman." She remained silent. "Can I see you tonight?"

She thought for a moment before replying, "Only if you promise to repeat that shower scene."

"Your wish is my command."

Now more than three years later and countless showers and secret meetings, she's still calling the shots.

EXCERPT FROM

The Alex Chronicles:
WHAT MY FRIENDS DON'T KNOW

Alex

I SCANNED THE ROOM ADMIRING the Who's Who of Atlanta, all here to help me celebrate the opening of my new store.

My cousin Taylor offered to throw me a welcome to Atlanta party, sort of a pre-opening. She said it's the best way to entice the glitterati of Atlanta to come to the opening. If I weren't the guest of honor, I'd be gone. I have so much to get done before the opening.

I looked across the room and caught the eye of the most beautiful man in the room. I convinced myself he was smiling at me, until I realized my cousin Taylor was behind me.

She walked over and whispered, "Too bad he is so old."

"How old is he?" I asked.

"He's in our neighborhood."

"So now, we're old?"

"No girl." She laughed. "You know what I mean. I thought I'd try something a little fresher." She turned to her right and cast a big smile in the direction of this young, honey colored, bald child standing in the corner. He was fine, but he still had milk on his lips. She motioned for him to come over although Mr. Dark Chocolate was also headed towards us.

Mr. Dark Chocolate moved like a gazelle, slow and steady gliding across the room. Swagger...confidence...danger. As he approached, I saw the details of his face more clearly. His skin looked like smooth dark chocolate and he had the most incredible light brown eyes. I've never seen a man so dark with such light eyes. They didn't seem real, nor did he. He smiled and I felt something deep in my core. I don't care if he's only coming over to talk to my cousin. I'm grateful to stand here in his presence and lust...I mean admire him. He stopped in front of us and my mind immediately filled with thoughts no good Christian girl should know anything about.I wonder what he looks like wet and naked. I looked around hoping I hadn't said that out loud.

"Hello, Taylor." He smiled.

Oh God, did You recycle Barry White's voice box and put it inside this beautiful package? My hormones and body went into a tailspin and I was ruined for any other man on this planet.

Taylor managed to pry herself from junior's arms long enough to acknowledge what I believe to be God's best work. "Hi Moses. I'm glad you came."

He kissed the back of her hand and replied, "Thank you for inviting me." He took my hand, turned it over and gently kissed it. I think my uterus just flipped over.

"Good evening, I'm Moses Adair."

Moses, lead me to the Promise land. "Alexandra Miller."

"Are you *the* Alex?" He asked.

If I wasn't, I was now. "Which Alex would that be?" I replied with a smile.

"The Alex I've been hearing people talk about all evening."

"Depends on what you've heard." I'm trying to flirt and that's not something I'm good at. I wanted to tell him, "I'm whoever I need to be in order to keep talking to you."

"Excuse me," Taylor said as she took junior's arm and left us standing in the middle of the room.

"I heard a woman say she hoped the pink dress Alex was wearing would be available at the store, because she liked the way it..." He slowly looked me up and down. When his eyes met mine, he was smiling. I instantly recognized that smile. It's the same one I had when I first spotted him. "...framed her face."

I gave him the same smile he gave me. "Then, I guess I am that Alex."

As soon as the flirting started, it ended. I saw him looking everywhere, but at me. Time to move on. I should have known this gorgeous man wasn't interested in me. I'm going to hurt Taylor for leaving me with one of her castoffs.

"Excuse me, but I…"

He gently grabbed my hand. "Please…" I looked at my hand and then his face. Those incredible eyes, went from light to dark brown in a matter of seconds. A jolt hit my core and I almost fell down. "Please…don't leave me alone."

"What?"

He leaned in close and his aftershave traveled up my nose. He smelled like an expensive cigar that had been dipped in plums and cardamon. I took a deep breath tattooing his scent in my mind. "May I tell you a secret?"

He can say anything he wants as long as I can hear that voice. I swallowed hard. "Sure."

"This really isn't my thing."

"Then why did you come?" He was still holding my hand. Part of me wanted him to let go before he realized how sweaty it was. The other part of me didn't ever want him to let it go. I looked down at my hand and back at him and he released my hand.

"I'm trying to be more outgoing. Meet new people."

"And how's that working out for you?" I asked with just enough sarcasm to be cute.

"I met one person so far," he joked.

"Uh-huh. Excuse me." I started walking away and he grabbed my wrist.

"I'm sorry, how long have you known Taylor?"

"She's my cousin, and you?"

"We dated briefly."

"Really?" I turned to face him.

"You sound surprised."

"I'm sorry, you just don't seem like her type." He looked across at Taylor and junior.

"I don't?"

"Did you know, when a woman meets a man, she can size him up in a matter of seconds."

"Really? Let's get a drink, while you explain women to me." He gently placed his hand on the small of my back and my body temperature tripled.

God, please let there be something wrong with him.

"What would you like?" he asked.

"A mineral water with lime."

"We'll both have mineral water. Thank you." He turned toward me and it felt like he was looking into my soul. I heard someone say, you know you've met the person you're supposed to be with when you look into their eyes and see all the generations you'll create. When I looked into his eyes, I saw our great grandchildren several times over. "You were saying?"

"It's simple. When a woman meets an attractive man, within thirty seconds, or less, she's picked out their china pattern, placed him at the altar, and given birth to their first child." The bartender placed my drink on the bar and nodded his head in agreement with me. "Thank you." I took a sip and continued. "He, on the other hand is just hoping she'll say hello."

"Thank you." He said to the bartender and took a sip of his drink. "Taylor doesn't strike me as that type."

"Taylor is the rule with a little exception. She can sum up if you're too old."

"Too old?" He looked surprised.

"Yeah, that's probably why it didn't work out between you two. She kind of has this thing for younger men." As soon as the words left my mouth, it hit me like a ton of bricks. Not only did I just betray my cousin, I just betrayed my sex and called him old. He looked at me and slowly turned his lips up into the most beautiful smile.

"Your insight is enlightening. However, I don't think that's why we stopped dating."

"Trust me."

"And here I thought it had to do with my wife."

"Your wife?"

THE ALEX CHRONICLES:
WHAT MY FRIENDS DON'T KNOW

AVAILABLE AT
WWW.READTRACYREED.COM

TRACY'S BOOKS

Generational Curse

The Alex Chronicles:
What My Friends Don't Know

The Good Girl

To sign up for Tracy Reed's
reader mailing list and to
receive news about new books, visit
www.readtracyreed.com

Made in the USA
Charleston, SC
17 October 2015